W9-BST-697

For Charlotte

Mister Horizontal
& Miss Vertical

Story by Noémie Révah
Illustrations by Olimpia Zagnoli
Translated from the French by Claudia Bedrick

ENCHANTED LION BOOKS
NEW YORK

Here is
Mister Horizontal.

Here is
Miss Vertical.

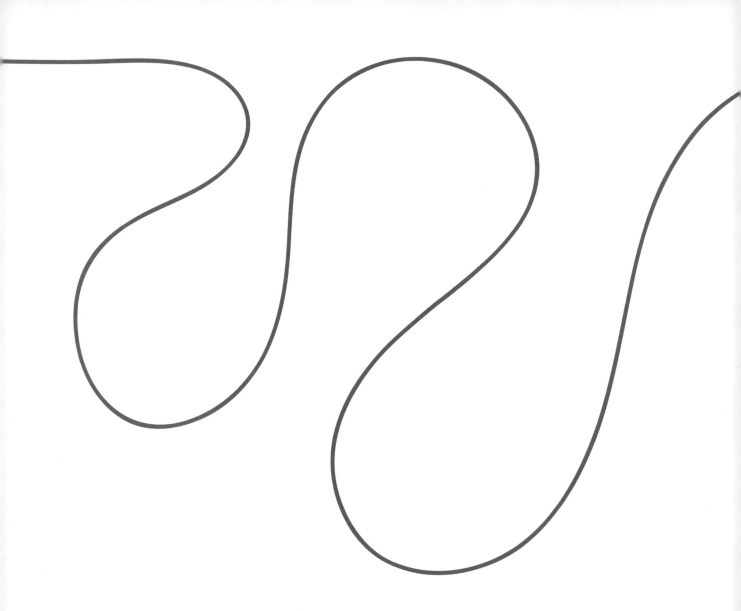

Mister Horizontal loves everything that glides. When he rollerblades on the bicycle path, he often dreams he's a great figure skater.

Miss Vertical loves launching herself into orbit and looping through the air.

She also loves propelling herself up, like a flea or a kangaroo.

Mister Horizontal likes to stretch, bend, and do funny somersaults.

He's a yoga expert.

Miss Vertical likes feeling dizzy
and often goes to the circus
to watch the acrobats perform
on the high wire.

Mister Horizontal likes water-skiing and boating, and always looks out at the horizon while floating on the waves.

Miss Vertical likes elevators. Going up and down in them is a big treat.

And she can often be
found on staircases.

He loves walking in the desert, with sand as far as the eye can see.

He could have been a camel driver in a caravan.

Sometimes she goes bungee jumping and dives off a cliff into thin air.

He likes ants and other insects that march in long lines.

She is crazy about rockets, which shoot her into space, toward the sun and the stars.

He likes a warm soak
in a big bathtub.

In the ocean, he floats
on his back while the fish
swim around him.

She loves New York, the city of skyscrapers.

She would make a great firefighter or window washer.

He likes to lounge and always stretches out when it's time for his nap.

She likes things that fly and carry her up into the sky.

She also loves floating weightlessly through the air.

He likes gardening and always plants his seeds in straight rows.

She likes to swing from trees like a monkey. High up in the branches, she talks with birds and koalas and gazes down at yellow jackets and butterflies.

He loves everything that zooms forward: scooters, bicycles, even motorcycles.

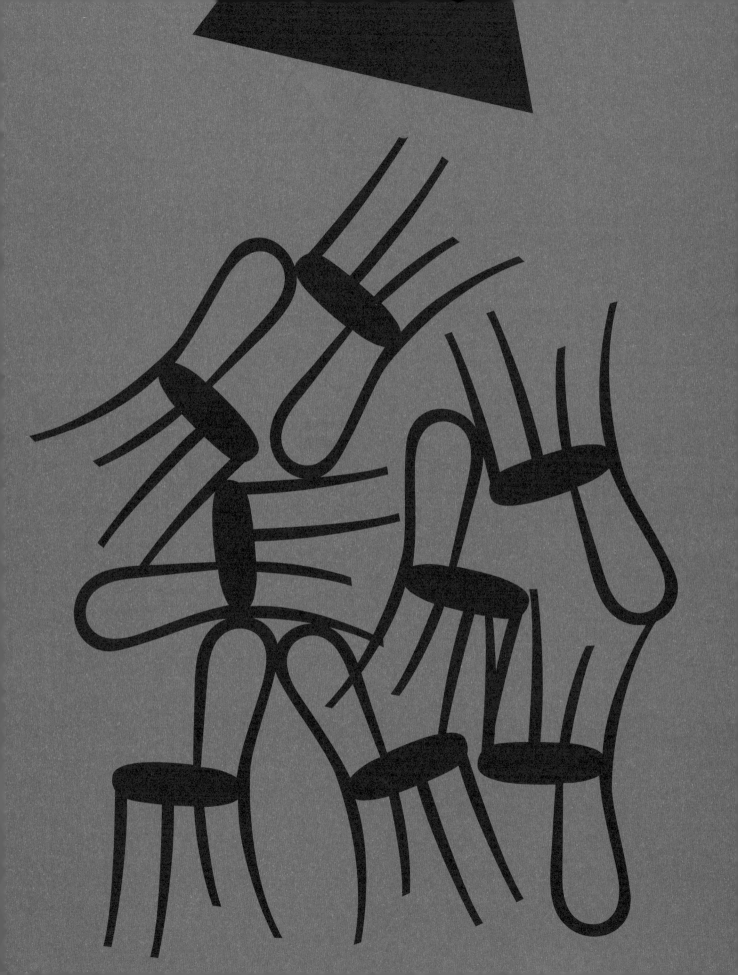

She collects ladders.

Even when she was small, as her parents recall, she stacked chairs up to the ceiling.

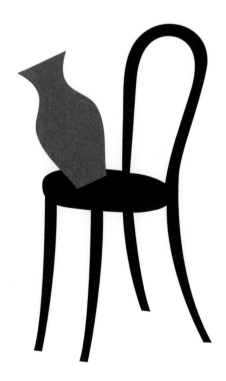

Now what do you think...

...their child will love?

With thanks to Michael, Mona, and Leo

www.enchantedlionbooks.com

First American edition published in 2014
by Enchanted Lion Books,
351 Van Brunt Street, Brooklyn, NY 11231

Originally published in France by Éditions Michel Lagarde, Paris.
Copyright © 2013 as *Monsieur Horizontal & Madame Verticale*
Copyright © 2014 by Enchanted Lion Books for the English-language edition
Graphic Design & Layout: fouinzanardi.com
With thanks to Sarah Klinger for her work on the translation.
All rights reserved under International and Pan-American Copyright Conventions.

ISBN 978-1-59270-161-2
Printed in May 2014 in China by the South China Printing Company.